Based on a story inspired by
Marshall Buehler

Story adapted by Ken Buehler. Written by Cheryl Skafte and Luke Moravec. Illustrations by Marissa Saurer. Produced by Josh Miller.
Version 1.2 of Christmas City Express

ISBN: 978-0-615-91628-6

I know this story is true because I was on that train,
the one they all talk about, the one they call the Christmas City Express.

It was a snowy Christmas Eve when I boarded that train to Duluth. Snowflakes were falling from the sky, tickling my nose, and collecting on top of my hat. At my feet was my father's old suitcase. Everything I needed was in there: enough clothes for the trip, a small platter of chocolate fudge to give to my grandfather, and a special gift for my grandmother - topped

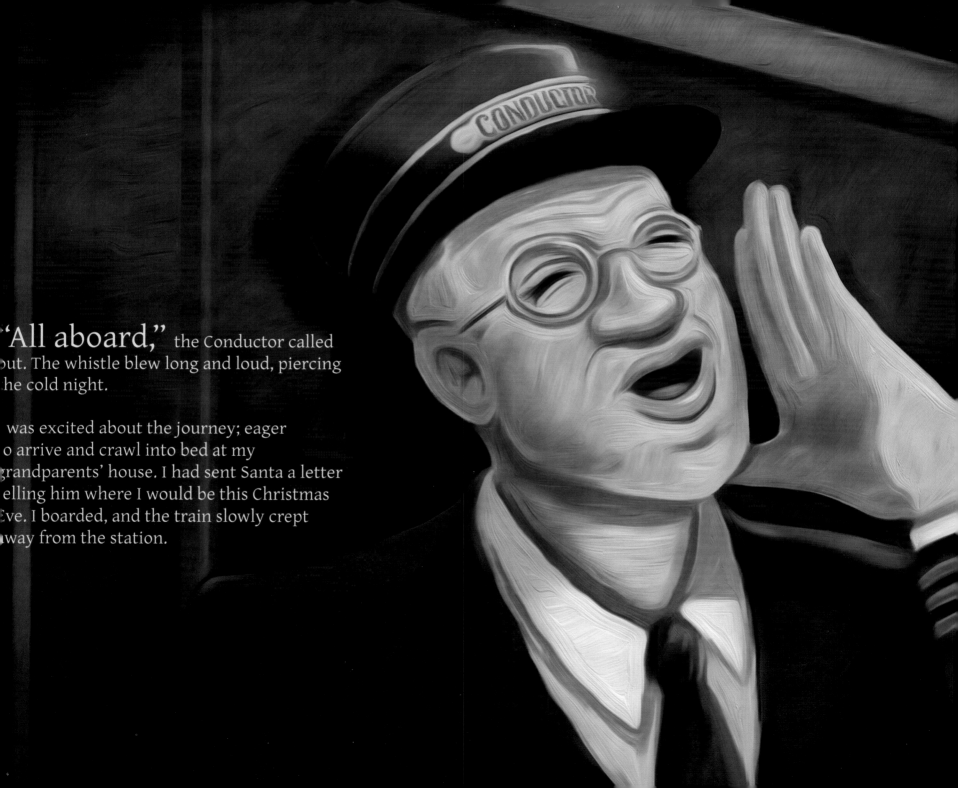

"All aboard," the Conductor called
out. The whistle blew long and loud, piercing
the cold night.

I was excited about the journey; eager
to arrive and crawl into bed at my
grandparents' house. I had sent Santa a letter
telling him where I would be this Christmas
Eve. I boarded, and the train slowly crept
away from the station.

The snow swirled and danced outside my window.

"Looks like the storm is picking up," said the Conductor, as he stopped to
check my ticket. The train traveled deep into the night. Outside, the tree branches, heavy with snow and ice,
looked like reindeer antlers. I thought about Santa's sleigh and wondered what gift he would leave for me under the tree.

I had just closed my eyes when the train wheels started to slow. The train gave a lurch. Then we stopped.

I peered out the window. The blizzard was blinding and the night was dark. The light from within the passenger car reflected
gently against the snow-blanketed hills. We were in the middle of nowhere; far from home, and far from our destination.

"Now, don't worry." The Conductor spoke loud enough for all the passengers to hear. "We have enough coal in the tender to keep us warm. But it appears that we'll be here all night."

"But we want to be home for Christmas," the passengers cried out. "We want to be with our families."

I was worried; maybe even a little scared. I didn't want to be late for my grandparents, and I didn't want to be stuck somewhere Santa couldn't find me. The Conductor checked his watch, looked at the unhappy passengers and then turned his

The Conductor grabbed his overcoat and lantern, and with a loud "harrumph" he headed outside.

I pressed my face against the cold window. I could just make out the lantern light as it bobbed and bounced into the distance. Then it disappeared. After a time, the dim light returned. The Conductor came into view. He was dragging something big behind him. There was a murmur from the passengers.

"What is that?" someone whispered.

"Maybe it's a mail bag," one man suggested.

"No, it's not," another person chimed in. "He's hauling someone's luggage behind him."

"I don't think he's carrying anything at all," said a woman across the aisle.
"It looks like a big black dog nipping at his heels!"

The passenger car was all abuzz when the Conductor appeared, empty handed, in the doorway.

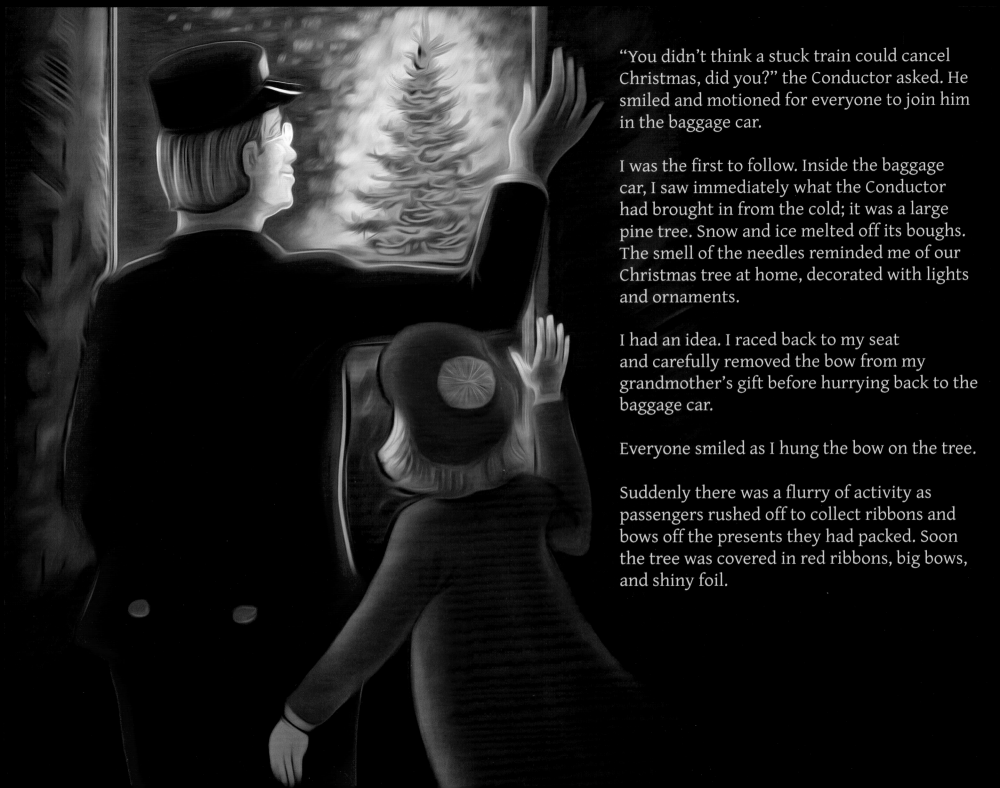

"You didn't think a stuck train could cancel Christmas, did you?" the Conductor asked. He smiled and motioned for everyone to join him in the baggage car.

I was the first to follow. Inside the baggage car, I saw immediately what the Conductor had brought in from the cold; it was a large pine tree. Snow and ice melted off its boughs. The smell of the needles reminded me of our Christmas tree at home, decorated with lights and ornaments.

I had an idea. I raced back to my seat and carefully removed the bow from my grandmother's gift before hurrying back to the baggage car.

Everyone smiled as I hung the bow on the tree.

Suddenly there was a flurry of activity as passengers rushed off to collect ribbons and bows off the presents they had packed. Soon the tree was covered in red ribbons, big bows, and shiny foil.

Laughter filled the train. A man with a deep voice started singing carols. A woman shared snowman-shaped cookies. The conductor heated up water on the train's boiler and made hot chocolate for everyone. The baggage car was warm, people were smiling and talking.

I was lost in thought, thinking about Santa flying around the sky looking for me, when a woman approached holding out a pair of knitted mittens. "I made these for my grandchild," she said. "I saw how you shared, and I'd like you to have them. Merry Christmas."

"Thank you," I said. As I tugged on the warm, fuzzy mittens, I realized that Christmas was here, right on the train. "I wish that everyone could get a gift on this Christmas night," I thought.

A big gust of wind unexpectedly shook the train. And then I heard it. It was quiet at first. It sounded like bells.

It sounded like jingle bells.

A loud thump sounded from the roof. Everyone looked up. Prancing footsteps echoed from above.

"What is that?" someone whispered.

"Maybe the storm is getting worse," one man suggested.

"No it's not," another person chimed in. "It must be one of the train engineers."

"I don't think it's that at all," said the woman who gave out the cookies. "Maybe a giant tree fell on the train!"

Everyone started talking at once, but they all fell silent when Santa Claus appeared in the doorway.

"I knew it was you," I whispered. He smiled.

"Well, I heard your wish." And with that, Santa handed me a gift. It was beautifully wrapped with colorful paper and a fancy ribbon. After each passenger had received a gift from Santa's bag, he turned to leave.

"Wait!" I called out. I found the bow I had tied to the tree and brought it to Santa. "It's not much, but you need a gift on Christmas too." As I placed the bow in Santa Claus's hand, soft and silent snowflakes started to magically fall from the ceiling of the baggage car, collecting at our feet.

"Merry Christmas to all and to all a good night!" Santa called out.

Then, as quickly as he had come, Santa was gone.

I reached down and picked up a snowflake. It was almost as big as my hand. The snowflake was cold to the touch, and – even aboard the warm train – showed no signs of melting.

While the other passengers opened their presents, I went to the window. The snow outside had stopped falling. The moon reflected her light on the sparkling silver and white hills. Santa's sleigh was a small dot in the sky, racing to its next location.

"Goodbye, Santa," I whispered.

I wearily made my way back to the passenger car.

With great care, I placed the snowflake in my suitcase before sleep closed my heavy eyes.

Early the next day, I woke to the sound of the train pulling into the Duluth Depot.
I saw my grandmother waving to me from the platform.

No one spoke of the events from the night before, and the Conductor ushered us all off the train with a smile and a tip of his ha

Since that day, I've told many people the story of my night on the Christmas City Express.

Most just shake their heads. I know they doubt its truth. I don't.

Every Christmas Eve, I open my father's old suitcase and hold in my hand a snowflake - cold to the touch and never melting.

About the Creators of the Christmas City Express

Illustrator

Co-Author *Co-Author*

Inspiratio

In addition to being an illustrator, Marissa, a life-long Minnesotan, is also a food photographer and chef. She enjoys outdoor adventures with her family, skiing and tennis. Her step daughter Micah has been incorporated into The Christmas City Express as one of the kids on board the train for that magical journey. She's the girl in green. Can you find her?

Cheryl Skafte was born and raised in Duluth, MN. Cheryl enjoys performing on local stages, teaching theater, and working with Duluth Parks and Recreation. If you would like to reach Cheryl and share your train story, please contact the Lake Superior Railroad Museum.

Luke Moravec is an artist from Duluth, MN. He works part-time as an after-school program coordinator, but finds plenty of moments for writing, reading, mountain biking, swimming in Lake Superior, and performing in theater and as a one-man band.

He is the dadibaajimoowinini. T story teller. Around the encampme fire of an Ojibwe village, the fam dinner table or at bedtime, Marsh Buehler was the one who broug the story. A memory, a tall tale yarn, he continues the time honor traditions of all people who carri the spoken word. This story is I favorite because it combines his lo for family, Christmas and TRAINS. volunteer on several tourist railroa Marshal enjoys the history of peo and the stories of railroads.